Piggies

Dedicated to Marjane Wood

Requests for permission to make copies of
any part of the work should be mailed to:
Permissions Department, Harcourt Brace & Company,
6277 Sea Harbor Drive, Orlando, Florida 32887-6777.

Library of Congress Cataloging-in-Publication Data
Wood, Don, 1945–
Piggies/Don and Audrey Wood; illustrated by Don Wood.
p.   cm.
Summary: Ten little piggies dance on a young child's
fingers and toes before finally going to sleep.
ISBN 0-15-256341-5
ISBN 0-15-200217-0 (pbk.)
[1. Bedtime — Fiction.   2. Games — Fiction.   3. Pigs — Fiction.]
I. Wood, Audrey.   II. Title.
PZ7.W84737P1   1991
[E] — dc20   89-24598

Printed in Singapore

B C D E F
A B C D E (pbk.)

The paintings in this book were done in oil on Bristol board.
The display type was set in Caxton Book.
The text type was set in Goudy Catalog.
Composition by Thompson Type, San Diego, California
Color separations were made by Bright Arts, Ltd., Singapore.
Printed and bound by Tien Wah Press, Singapore
Production supervision by Warren Wallerstein and Michele Green
Designed by Michael Farmer

Piggies

WRITTEN BY

Don and Audrey Wood

ILLUSTRATED BY

Don Wood

A Voyager Book

Harcourt Brace & Company

SAN DIEGO   NEW YORK   LONDON

I've got two

fat little piggies,

two smart

little piggies,

two   long

little piggies,

two silly

little piggies,

and two wee

little piggies.

Sometimes they're

hot little piggies,

and sometimes they're

cold little piggies.

Sometimes they're

clean little piggies,

and sometimes they're

dirty little piggies.

Sometimes they're

good little piggies,

but not at bedtime. That's when

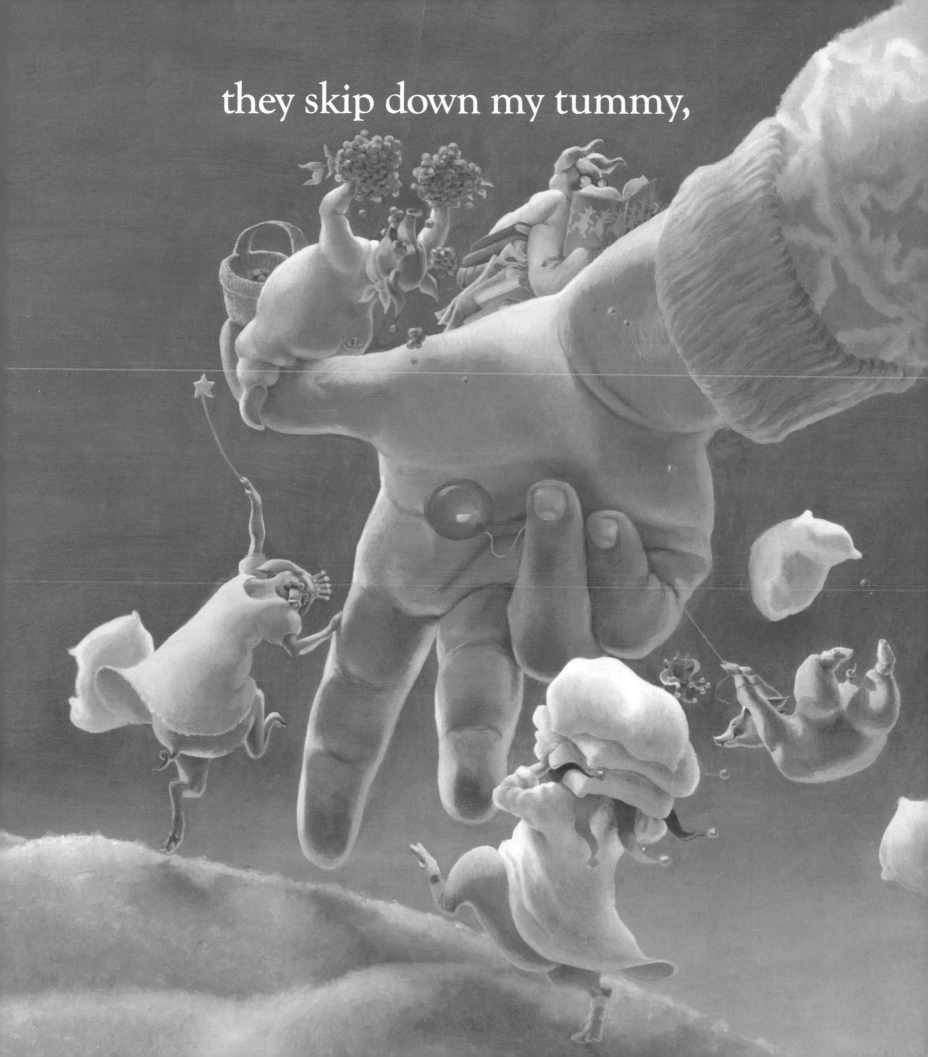

they skip down my tummy,

dance on my toes,

then run away and hide.

So . . .

. . . I put them together, all in a row,
for two fat kisses,
two smart kisses,
two long kisses,
two silly kisses,

and two wee kisses goodnight.